Way Out in the
Desert

Way Out in the Desert

by *T. J.* Marsh *and* Jennifer Ward

illustrated by
Kenneth J. Spengler

rising moon
Books for Young Readers from Northland Publishing

The illustrations were rendered in gouache on watercolor paper
The text type was set in Skia
The display type was set in Quetzelcoatl
Composed in the United States of America
Designed by Rudy J. Ramos
Production by Billie Jo Bishop
Edited by Tom Carpenter and Erin Murphy
Production supervised by Lisa Brownfield
Printed in Hong Kong by Wing King Tong Company Limited

FIRST IMPRESSION, March 1998
ISBN 0-87358-687-5

Special Scholastic Book Fair Edition, December 1998
ISBN 0-87358-738-3

Marsh, T. J., date.
Way out in the desert / by T.J. Marsh and Jennifer Ward ;
illustrated by Kenneth J. Spengler.
p.   cm.
Summary: A counting book in rhyme presents various desert animals
and their children, from a mother horned toad and her little toadie
one to a mom tarantula and her little spiders ten. Numerals are
hidden in each illustration.
ISBN 0-87358-687-5
[1. Desert animals—Fiction. 2. Animals—Infancy—Fiction.
3. Counting. 4. Picture puzzles. 5. Stories in rhyme.]   I. Ward,
Jennifer, date. II. Spengler, Kenneth, ill. III. Title.
PZ8.3.M393Way 1998
[E]—dc21   97-47220

To my rhyming angels, Tierney and Riley,
for filling my days with wonder and joy.

—T. J. M.

For Kelly, my inspiration.—J.W.

Hey, kids!
Look for the number
hidden on each page!

Way out in the desert having fun in the sun

lived a mother horned toad and her little toady one.

"Scurry!" said the mother. "I scurry!" said the one,

so they scurried all morning having fun in the sun.

Way out in the desert where the wildflowers grew

lived a mother hummingbird and her little hummers two.

"Sip!" said the mother. "We sip!" said the two,

so they sipped and they dipped where the wildflowers grew.

3

Way out in the desert by the palo verde tree

lived a mother javelina and her little piggies three.

"Snooze!" said the mother. "We snooze!" said the three,

'cause they rooted all night by the palo verde tree.

Way out in the desert near the ocotillo door

lived a rattlesnake mother and her baby snakes four.

"Rattle!" said the mother. "We rattle!" said the four,

so they rattled in the shadow of the ocotillo door.

Way out in the desert where the cactus bloom and thrive

lived a mother Gila monster and her little monsters five.

"Burrow!" said the mother. "We burrow!" said the five,

so they burrowed and they dug where the cactus bloom and thrive.

Way out in the desert in a nest built of sticks

lived a mother roadrunner and her little chicks six.

"Run!" said the mother. "We run!" said the six,

so they ran chasing lizards near their nest built of sticks.

Way out in the desert where saguaros reach to heaven
lived a mother jackrabbit and her little jacks seven.
"Snuggle!" said the mother. "We snuggle!" said the seven,
so they snuggled all night where saguaros reach to heaven.

Way out in the desert on the old corral gate

lived an old scorpion mother and her little scorpions eight.

"Hold on!" said the mother. "We'll hold on!" said the eight,

so they rode on her back up the old corral gate.

Way out in the desert where the moon shone fine

lived a mother coyote and her little pups nine.

"Howl!" said the mother. "We howl!" said the nine,

so they howled and they barked while the moon shone fine.

Way out in the desert in a prickly pear den
lived a mom tarantula and her little spiders ten.
"Spin!" said the mother. "We spin!" said the ten,
so they spun all night in their prickly pear den.

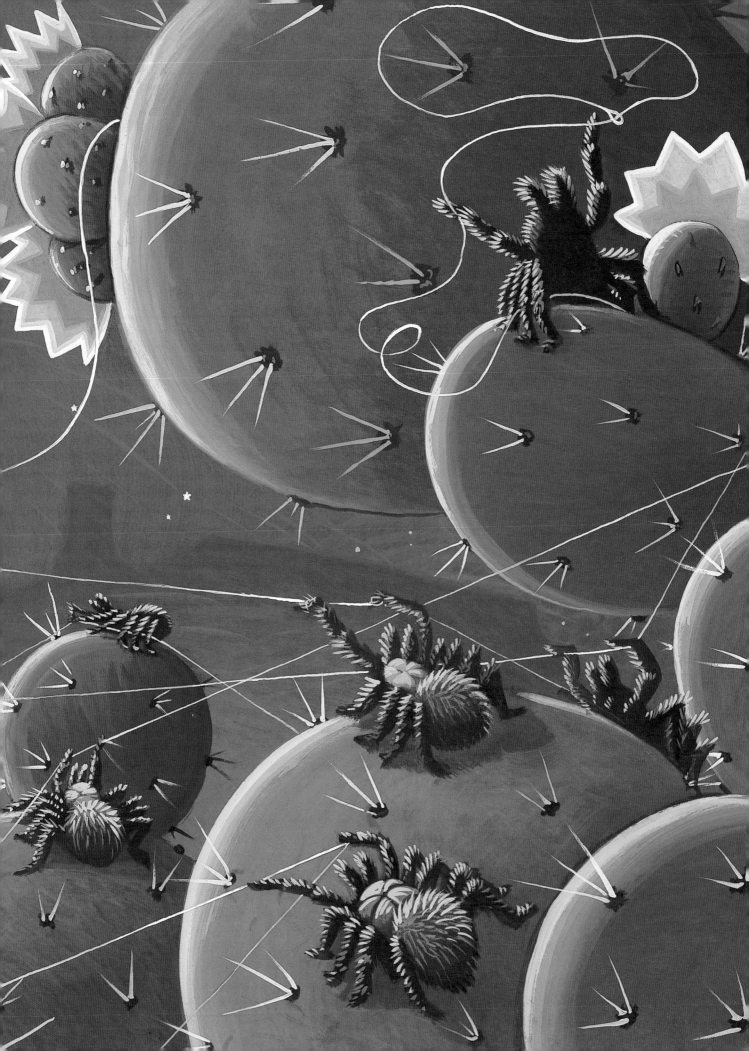

Glossary

burrow — To escape the intense heat of the desert, many animals dig into the ground, where it is much cooler. This is called burrowing. The hole they dig is called a burrow.

cactus — This large group of plants has learned to survive in the desert by storing water in their trunks. Over time, leaves have changed to spines to protect stored water from thirsty animals.

coyote — An extremely adaptable animal, the coyote can be a predator, scavenger, or vegetarian. Although coyotes are often seen during the day, on a night with a full moon, their barks, yips, yelps, and growls can nearly always be heard out in the desert.

desert — A desert is a dry region that receives less than ten inches of rain per year. Deserts can be either hot or cold. Most people think of deserts as being barren, but deserts of the Southwest, especially the Sonoran, are very lush, with many plants and animals.

Gila monster — Gila (hee-la) monsters aren't monsters at all, they're lizards. They are poisonous, but they don't have fangs. Their venom flows down the grooves of their back teeth each time they bite down.

hummingbird — There are three different types of hummingbirds that nest in the Sonoran desert. A hummingbird lays two eggs in a nest made out of plant material and spider webs. The webs allow the nest to stretch as the baby birds grow. These busy little birds consume half their weight in insects and nectar each day.

horned toad —The desert horned toad is really a lizard that looks like a toad. It even eats like a toad by shooting out its long, sticky tongue to capture ants.

jackrabbit —Jackrabbits aren't really rabbits at all, but are considered hares. Hares are different from rabbits because their babies are born fully furred and with their eyes open. Jackrabbits' very large ears help keep them cool, since they spend all of their time on the desert's surface, where it can become very hot indeed. Jackrabbits do not burrow; instead, they scratch out small areas under desert shrubs for shelter.

javelina (hav-uh-LEE-na)—Also known as collared peccaries, javelinas are nocturnal (active at night) and travel in groups of up to thirty animals. They eat shrubs, nuts, fruit, roots, and cactus—spines and all.

ocotillo (O-koh-TEE-yo)—These beautiful plants look like seaweed in the desert landscape. They are sometimes called "living fences" because cut pieces, stuck in the ground as fence posts, will frequently grow roots and sprout blossoms on the top!

palo verde tree —*Palo verde* is Spanish for "green wood." This special tree of the desert has a green trunk and green branches. It has very small, thin leaves. The green stuff in the leaves of plants makes food for the plants. During times of drought, this tree loses first its leaves, then its twigs, and sometimes even its branches, yet can still produce food for itself because of the green in its trunk.

prickly pear—Prickly pears are also called beavertail cactus. Many animals love the fruit, called *tunas,* which people sometimes make into delicious syrup, jelly, and candy.

rattlesnake—Rattlesnakes are timid creatures that use venom to quiet the animals they eat, like mice and rabbits, so the prey can't hurt them. Like many other snakes, the rattlesnake shakes its tail when it is scared. Luckily for us, it has a rattle on the end of its tail, so we usually get plenty of warning to get out of the way! Most snakes lay eggs, but rattlesnakes give birth to fully-formed young.

roadrunner—This is a bird that would rather run than fly. Roadrunners lay three to six eggs in saucer-shaped nests in mesquite bushes, large cactus, or shrubs. They feed on lizards, snakes, and insects.

saguaro (sa-WAR-oh)— In May, this giant cactus blooms beautiful white flowers that bloom only one night. Woodpeckers drill into the trunk of the saguaro and build their nests inside, where it is cool and sheltered. When the woodpeckers move out, all sorts of animals move in, and it doesn't hurt the saguaro at all!

scorpion —The most common scorpion is the giant hairy desert scorpion, although there are at least thirty different species that live in the Sonoran Desert. Scorpions give birth to babies that immediately climb onto their mothers' backs, where they live for a week or two until they shed their skin for the first time. Most scorpion stings are not fatal, but they are painful!

tarantula —The nocturnal tarantula hunts for bugs near its burrow. It can't see very well, so it often spins a line of silk to find its way home. Even though they look scary, these gentle spiders almost never bite. Many people who live in the desert keep them as pets.

wildflowers —The Sonoran Desert's wildflower season lasts all year. This may be because the desert's definition of a wildflower is very generous, including herbs, trees, cactus, and shrubs, all of which produce flowers in a rainbow of colors.

Your mom and dad may have sung "Over in the Meadow" when they were children—and probably your grandma and grandpa did, too! It was written more than one hundred years ago by Olive A. Wadsworth.

Here in the Sonoran Desert, we would have to go a long way to find a meadow. We decided to write new words to the tune of "Over in the Meadow" so we could sing about the plants and animals in our own backyards. We hope you enjoy learning all about them!

Way Out in the Desert

Way out in the des-ert hav-ing fun in the sun lived a moth-er horned toad and her lit-tle toa-dy one. "Scurry!" said the moth-er. "I scur-ry!" said the one, so they scur-ried all morn-ing hav-ing fun in the sun.

T. J. MARSH is an aerospace engineer, scuba diver, pilot, and world traveler. When she moved to the Sonoran Desert, she fell in love with the incredible plants and animals she found there. She lives in Tucson, Arizona, with her husband, Phil, and daughters Riley and Tierney.

JENNIFER WARD is an elementary school teacher who has lived in the Sonoran Desert for twelve years. She and her husband, Richard, and their daughter, Kelly, live in Tucson.

KENNETH J. SPENGLER began his career as an illustrator shortly after he graduated from Tyler School of Art with a B.F.A., and his work can be found on anything from posters to billboards, from mystery covers to children's books such as *How Jackrabbit Got His Very Long Ears* and *A Campfire for Cowboy Billy,* both from Rising Moon.